Santa the Covid Christmas Crisis!

Fi Star-Stone

Copyright © 2020 Fi star-Stone

All rights reserved.

ISBN:9798689131818

For my little awesome duo - Betsy and Oscar, who have been asking me to write a children's book for so long.

'Seeing is believing, but sometimes the most real things in the world are the things we can't see.'

The Conductor - The Polar Express

MY THINKY-THOUGHTS JOURNAL

Name: Eliza Greenwood

Age: $10\frac{1}{2}$

Hobbies: Drawing, Movies, Music, reading, Football, Playing guitar and anything Art.

Likes: Chocolate, Sweets, my pets, my family.

Dislikes: Mushrooms and onions.

When I grow up I want to be: A doctor or maybe a footballer.

November 30th 2020

Bad start to what turned out to be THE WORST DAY ON EARTH!

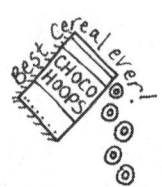

Firstly, we ran out of choco-hoops for breakfast, so had to have toast and I *MAY* have grumbled quite a bit.

Mum said I should be *"thankful we have food at all young lady, because some don't have any food at all!"*

How to make me feel R U B B I S H in one sentence. Thanks Mum.

Then I couldn't find my unicorn pen from Biggle - my FAVOURITE EVER shop. Turns out Victor 'needed' it for his game of Dragons. "LOST it! Soz!" He said.

Mum said "sharing is caring Eliza - I really am disappointed with your attitude lately!"

Victor NEVER gets told off. Well, O.K — that's a lie. He does, often, but not today, and he should because you don't borrow things without asking. Am I right? Or am I RIGHT? (And I know you read my diary Victor - SO DON'T BORROW MY STUFF WITHOUT ASKING AGAIN!)

I arrived at school late. Miss Jolly the deputy head was far from jolly. She was in a really bad mood (again.)

It meant I missed 10 minutes of morning break because *'if you come to school ten minutes late Eliza Greenwood, then I will take those ten minutes back from your playtime!'*

 Seems fair. N O T!

Roll on past DOUBLE MATHS and P.E, to last playtime where...

THE WORST THING
IN THE WORLD HAPPENED...

Which officially made today...

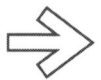   **THE WORST DAY
ON EARTH!**

Sarah Thomas has always been on my list of **'people I am not very keen on'** and although my mum says,

'Eliza - be kind to mean people, as they are the ones that need it most.'
I find it SO hard to WANT

to be kind to her.

And now...

After today...

I don't think I will ever want to be kind to her ever again.

Sarah Thomas just ruined Christmas.

I mean, it was already going to totally suck with the whole Covid situation going on, meaning the school Christmas party was cancelled but...

Today, Sarah-Christmas-magic crusher-Thomas, UPPED that 'rubbish Christmas' to a whole new level.

We are now on level **'don't-even-bother-hanging-your-stocking-kids!'**

Why? Well, because Sarah told the whole of 5B that Santa isn't real, because Kelly in our class, 6T, told her so.

SANTA!!!

THE Santa! Also known as Father Christmas, the guy in RED, the Magical guy that brings surprises for your stocking after flying through the sky... SANTA!

YUP. She Told EVERYONE in 5B (and consequently the whole of our school!)

Heart. Broken.
DREAMS ALL SHATTERED TO A MILLION PIECES.

☆ONE RUBBISH - THREE AWESOMES☆

One rubbish thing about today:

THE WORST THING EVER IN THE WORLD HAPPENED!

Three AWESOME things about today:

1. Nothing

2. Nothing

3. Nothing

December 1st 2020

Today started well. Not only did mum get more choco-hoops - she also surprised me and Victor with ADVENT CALENDARS! It's a bittersweet treat. Dad always bought the Advent calendars and so it makes me remember and miss him even more.

Victor got a 'Star Fighter 2020' one and I got...

☆THE BRAND NEW AWESOME 2020 BIGGLE CALENDAR! ☆

I don't know how I'm going to stop myself from opening every single door RIGHT NOW, because I LOVE stationary so much - even more than I love cake. True story.

Year 4 got sent home today because someone in their 'bubble' got Covid, it is making me feel so scared, but it also makes me feel really angry because it's changed my life loads. I hate it.

If Covid were a person I'd punch it on the nose even though Mum always says,

"Violence is never the answer Eliza. Words are more powerful. Always use your words not your fists!"

Nice thinking Mum, but I don't think Covid would politely refrain from making everyone sick, if I just asked it to... Nope!

I would punch it in it's sticky face! **K A P O W !**

Apart from absolutely hating Covid, I'm still absolutely hating Sarah for what she told everyone yesterday.

I'm also half not believing her. She has a long history of telling enormous lies. Last week she told us she was related to the Queen and that she  goes for dinner LOADS!

 She also told us she was travelling to L.A, to stay at SIMONE COWELLY'S mansion, because Simone is best friends with her mum. So you see? Not the most trustworthy source of information.

My bestie, Amalie said *"of course she*

is lying Eliza! I had a video call from Santa last year and it was amazing!"

Victor says he still believes in Santa because he really wants "The Star fighter 92 machine for Christmas and if you don't believe in him Eliza - then he won't come!"

Mum said 'Eliza darling, you can't always see the things you believe in - and that's half the magic. Some people don't believe in certain things and that's OK! Only you can decide!"

Christmas sure is going to be rubbish this year. No parties, no big family gatherings and no Dad again. This will be the second year without him.

Dad LOVED Christmas. So do I. Well, I did until now.

☆ONE RUBBISH - THREE AWESOMES☆

One rubbish thing about today:

Year 4 got sent home - it's made me really worried about Covid again, just as things felt like they were getting back to normal.

Three AWESOME things about today:

1. Awesome Calendar

2. Video call with Amalie

3. Mum has given me a little hope that Sarah is in fact a BIG LIE BAG!

December 2nd 2020

Double Geography with Mr Lake today and I almost fell asleep in class. That'll teach me staying up way-past 'lights out' to finish the latest Jack Wilton book! I love his books! I love reading and escaping into a story.

Mum asked me and Victor at breakfast, to write our Santa 'wish list' letters. We've been leaving our wish-list notes for Santa by the fireplace since we were teeny. Mum says when we couldn't actually write - we'd scribble or draw as Santa always translates wishes, even if grown-ups themselves can't read them. I love that.

The thing is... I'm not sure I want to write to Santa if what Sarah says is true. What's the point if he never gets to read it?

Mum says sometimes kids my age get doubtful about Santa and that's O.K.

She says she will always believe in Santa, just like Dad did and that it's just not Christmas without a little magic.

I hate it when the doubt cloud fills my head. It sometimes happens at football or school - I start being doubtful of how good I am during a match, or how smart I am in a maths test, then I feel totally rubbish about myself and get sweaty and hot.

Mum says,

"It's OK to have these feelings Eliza - they are normal! It's how you deal with those feelings that matters!

*So - Blow away the doubt cloud!
Take a BIG*

      DEEP

            BREATH....

Then blow it out and you'll feel better!"

So, I do what mum says - and you know what? It really works.

I feel better.
I feel a little hopeful.

So, I get my pencil and paper out and I start to write Santa a very
different letter
this year...

☆ONE RUBBISH - THREE AWESOMES☆

One rubbish thing about today:

The doubt cloud made an appearance again.

Three AWESOME things about today:

1. I used Mum's clever idea to blow the doubt cloud away and it left me feeling so much better.

2. I remembered all the lovely notes we'd left for Santa over the years when Dad was here.

3. I've started my letter to Santa.

December 3rd 2020

Screen-ban all day, for throwing my neatly ironed laundry pile in the cupboard instead of putting it away. Harsh!

This means no video chat to Amalie after school, no 'MyTube' unboxing videos and no episodes of my fave baking show. Being 10½ sucks sometimes.

Mum said *"I'm so disappointed Eliza! I took the time to wash and iron your clothes, it's not much to ask you to put them away! At your age I was doing the washing AND ironing and never complained!"*

This makes me feel **level 10** bad. I say sorry, but the screen-ban remains.

Of course perfect Victor put all his away and took great pleasure in smiling at me, behind mum's back, while she told me off. Urgh. Brothers are totally RUBBISH.

Year 4 are still in isolation. As worrying as it is - playtime is pretty awesome at the minute. We have the hang-out benches all to ourselves, and the playtime equipment, it is SO brilliantly quiet.

I mean, I do feel awful that some families are poorly and I'm super-worried we will get it too, BUT I kinda like having the school a little quieter.

Mum says that the poorly kids in year 4 are actually doing O.K. That their symptoms are mild and we shouldn't worry, but I am still worried. What if I lost Mum too. I've written my letter to Santa. I think it's my best EVER!

Dear Santa,

I'm 10½ now and I've been writing to you every year since I was tiny.

Anyway - thing is Santa, someone at our school (Sarah Thomas if you want to put her on the naughty list,) has told EVERYONE that you're not actually real. I know right?
A first I believed her, but then, after talking to my best friend and my mum, I don't think I believe her totally - but I do have a few doubts.

So, I have a few questions to check out if you are actually real or not. I know you are busy at this time of year, but if you could get back to me I'd really appreciate it.

If you can answer the questions on the next page and send them back to me - it would help me, believe in you, more.
                Love Eliza xx

1. How do you know the names and addresses of ALL the kids in the world?
2. How do you get around the world in one night?
3. How do you know who's been bad or good?
4. How do you get into house that don't have a Chimney?
5. Why do people say you aren't real?
6. What happens if you stop believing?
7. Why don't you shave?
8. Can your reindeer really fly?
9. What about Covid? Is it safe for you to come into our home and all the homes around the world? It's a global pandemic after all!
10. Why do some kids get lots of toys at Christmas and others not-so-much?
11. If you really are magic - can you make my Dad come back to us, just for one day?

That's it! Please reply as soon as possible.

December 4th 2020

I dreamt about dad last night. We were sledging down the big hill near our house and laughing. So much laughing. There used to be so much laughter in our house but since dad died it's not the same. (I H-A-T-E the words DEATH and DIED by the way. They make me get a big lump in my throat and feel all hot and red and angry.)

I've told mum about the letter and she smiled. Tonight after school we had hot chocolate with marshmallows and squirty cream, and and put our letters by the fireplace.

School was ace today. Friday is my favourite day at school because it's FISH AND CHIPS FRIDAY and our school cook is awesome!

He makes the best mushy peas in the whole entire world. Hardly anyone at school likes them, so me and Victor (who take after dad and LOVE them,) always get double helpings. YUMMY!

Friday's have the best lessons too! Double English with Mr Michaels, Art with Mrs Murray, and DT with Mr Masood! EPIC!

Sarah is in everyones bad-books, nobody will play with her at break, or sit next to her at lunch. The whole school are talking about Santa and and

and discussing if he's real or not. Sarah's parents were called into school after lots of complaints from parents. I couldn't help but giggle, seeing her go into the head teachers office with her parents at lunchtime was so funny, her face was all sour.

Mum said *"Eliza - everybody makes mistakes and it is better to live a life of kindness and to forgive, than to carry hate with you everywhere!"*

I guess it is the season of goodwill, I guess Sarah was only repeating what heard and I guess she ruined her own Christmas too? I'll think about it.

Speaking of goodwill, Victor found my unicorn pen and returned it with a note saying how sorry he was. Maybe he's not so bad after all.

☆ONE RUBBISH - THREE AWESOMES☆

One rubbish thing about today:

Woke up thinking about Dad and how much I miss him.

Three AWESOME things about today:

1. Fish and chips FRIDAY!

2. Sarah Thomas had to go see the headteacher WITH HER PARENTS! Ultimate walk of shame! Brilliant.

3. Victor found my pen and we put our letters to Santa by the fireplace before bed! (O.K, I snuck in an extra 'awesome' today - but it's been a GOOD day!

December 5th 2020

TWENTY DAYS UNTIL CHRISTMAS!

I am so excited and happy because today we went up to the forestry commission and chose our tree!

Dad always LOVED a real tree, but mum always said they made too much mess with the needles dropping all over the floor, and our dogs knocking the tree every minute, meant it was usually a bald tree by Christmas eve!

On Dad's last Christmas with us, he said we HAD to get a real one. It made a HUGE mess, but mum didn't care. She promised him we'd always keep getting real ones. That made dad happy. She has kept her promise even though it is hard doing it without Dad, and his choosing and carrying and getting-it-into-the-car skills!

It's in the garden at the moment to *"stand for a bit"* says Mum. *"Then tomorrow we can bring it in and decorate it!"*

Today (Saturday) is 'chores day' which bores me to tears, but mum always seems to make it fun.

Mum said *"We all live in this house Eliza and we all play a part in keeping it tidy and clean! It doesn't have to be boring you know?"* And with that she put on our favourite Christmas playlist and cranked up the volume really LOUD.

We all danced around doing our jobs. Mum cleaned the bathroom, Victor did vacuuming and I was on kitchen duty.

Victor and I get pocket money for helping too. We get £3 each week and I've saved up £15 now, to spend in the 'Biggle January sale' after Christmas. Mum likes my 'thrifty budget planning!' and always says dad would be really proud!

Victor spends his every week on sweets at Mr Timms shop in town. Mum pops in for him on her way home from work. I think Victor will be toothless by the time he's 12.

In the afternoon we watched a Christmas movie and it was one that always makes mum cry. (To be fair - mum cries at most things on the telly, even the adverts!) The big stores all have a big Christmas advert competition every year and Mum just sobs her way through them.

Today's movie was one of Dad's favourites,

'It's a Wonderful Life!'

It makes me cry, not because it was sad but with a mushy ending, but because I really miss Dad.

Amalie and I had a video-call again today. She says she still **fully** believes in Santa and wishes Sarah had never said that stupid thing at school.

Amalie is VERY worried about Santa and the whole Covid situation. I am too. We've decided it's best not to worry until we've heard back from Santa himself.

She also says she has asked for a new scooter for Christmas. She wants a pink one with glitter and ribbons on the handles. Or she wants a 'style doll.'

I really want one too but some of the mean girls in my old school said I'm too old for dolls. I told them,

"Well you're too young for make-up and smart-phones so between us we are about even!"

Mum said *"I do agree with you Eliza, but just because someone puts you down - it doesn't mean you should put them down in return. We all make our own choices in life and should respect those around us, as long as they are not hurting us with their choices."*

Mum always seems to know just what to say. Sometimes it's wonderful - and sometimes it's just SO infuriating! But she's always right.

Victor has been mostly annoying today because mum says Covid restrictions mean we can't have friends over.

Victor wants to play with Arthur **SO** badly, so has spent the day stropping and moaning and begging and tantruming. Mum says the rules and restrictions are there to protect us all.

Tonight we were allowed to stay up to watch star-factor, which finished at 9.30pm! Late nights are the BEST - especially with hot chocolate and cream. It's the end to a really nice day. I do wish Dad was here though.

☆ONE RUBBISH - THREE AWESOMES☆

One rubbish thing about today:

Missing Dad

Three AWESOME things about today:

1. We got our tree! It's so big and beautiful and smells incredible!

2. Video call with Amalie

3. Staying up late!

December 6th 2020

O-M-Gosh!!!

I got a letter today...

From SANTA CLAUS...

Not...

Even...

Joking...

LOOK!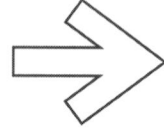

Santa Claus Lane,
North Pole,
Alaska 99705.

Dear Miss Greenwood,

Many thanks for your letter.

Father Christmas is incredibly busy at this time of year but has asked me to pass on his best wishes to you.

On the next pages are the answers to your questions. I hope they help. Santa looks forward to delivering surprises to your stocking on Christmas Eve! Merry Christmas!

Best wishes,

Duke

- Head Elf

Santa Claus Lane,
North Pole,
Alaska 99705.

1. We know the names and addresses of ALL the children in the world as they are in Santa's magical book.

2. Santa gets around in the world in one night by MAGIC and by using time zones to his advantage! He starts by delivering presents at the International Date Line and travels West following the Earth's rotation around the sun. By doing this, he gains extra hours of time. Children are actually waking up and opening presents while Santa is still delivering to others!

3. We know who has been 'bad or good' by looking in Santa's big red magical book! It updates daily. All children are good really though, we know that everyone has bad days sometimes, even grown-ups, so if you've had a few bad days try not to worry!

Santa Claus Lane,
North Pole,
Alaska 99705.

4. Santa can get into houses without chimneys by using magic! Santa also has a magical key that opens most doors.

5. Some say Santa isn't real because they find it hard to believe in something they can't actually see - and that's OK! We are all free to believe what we want to believe.

6. If people stop believing it doesn't mean Santa isn't real. He lives in the hearts of everyone at Christmas and that magic never dies, even when you are all grown up. Have you ever known a Christmas without Santa?

7. Santa likes his beard - he's had it for hundreds of years. It also keeps his face warm when flying on a cold Christmas eve.

Santa Claus Lane,
North Pole,
Alaska 99705.

8. Reindeer can only fly with magic.

9. Santa is super safe and also magical - this horrid Coronavirus doesn't affect him. However, Santa is going to be extra-careful when it comes to delivering gifts this year so don't worry.

Make sure you keep yourself safe too - do lots of hand washing and use hand sanitiser as you don't want to get poorly.

10. Santa delivers mostly what parents or carers can afford to buy, together with a few of his own surprises. Not everyone has the same amount of money - so some children have more gifts than others. Remember, the true magic of Christmas is giving - so if you want to help Santa out, you could wrap a small gift to donate to a local charity for families who don't have very much. That would be really kind!

Santa Claus Lane,
North Pole,
Alaska 99705.

11. Santa knows how very hard it is to lose someone you love very much. He would give anything to be able to grant this wish - but sadly it isn't something Santa can do.

Santa has magic, but he can't change the way of life or the way of the world, otherwise he would make sure all the bad things in the world stopped happening and that this horrid virus was gone.

Santa wants you to know that even though your dad has sadly passed away - he still lives on in you always. Every time you think of a happy memory - he is right there in your heart and therefor with you always.

I honestly never EVER thought I'd get a letter back answering all of my questions. I'd never thought about Dad like Santa says. I like that.

Wait til' I tell Sarah Thomas! I cannot wait to see her silly face go bright red and look utterly stupid for saying such a

GREAT

BIG

LIE!

Today is a BRILLIANT day.

I am SO happy.

☆ONE RUBBISH - THREE AWESOMES☆

One rubbish thing about today:

NOTHING!!!

Three AWESOME things about today:

1. A LETTER FROM SANTA (well, his elf!)

2. We decorated the tree today - it looks so pretty!

3. SANTA IS **REAL!**

December 7th 2020

BAD DAY! I've got to do detention **every** playtime this week at school.

Mum is NOT happy.

Mum said *"I am so disappointed Eliza - I have told you so many times my thoughts on violence. It is NEVER the answer. What would Dad say?"*

I made it worse saying *"Dad wouldn't say anything because he's dead!"* And then mum cried and wouldn't stop crying and now I feel **so so so so so** horrid and I'm not even using commas as I write this, so Mr Michaels my English teacher would be disappointed too... I am writing it all down so fast to get it off my chest...

OH PERFECT...

Here comes THE DOUBT CLOUD...

Thanks very much for that, you horrid doubt cloud! I feel awful about myself. Thing is - it wasn't even MY fault! (OK, so the pushing Sarah into the school pond bit - that WAS my fault,) but the reason why I did it was SARAH DREAM-CRUSHER's fault!!!

 I was so happy yesterday when I got the letter. (SO happy!)

I could not wait to show all the kids at school my amazing letter, (which I forgot to mention yesterday was full of wonderful glitter!) I knew they would all feel so much better, that like me, they would all believe again and then Sarah...

Oh gosh I can feel myself getting angry and hot again...

Deep...

Breath...

in...

and

Blow

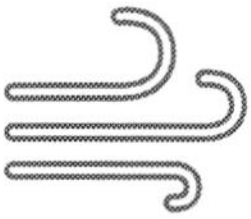

That
    A
     N
      G
       E
       R
         Away....

So...

I waited until first break to show my letter, because Mr Marvin doesn't like us chatting or doing show-and-tell first thing.

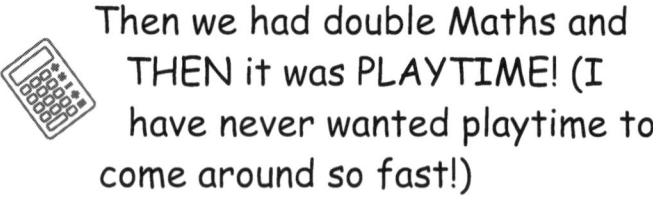

Then we had double Maths and THEN it was PLAYTIME! (I have never wanted playtime to come around so fast!)

I ran to the playground - letter firmly gripped in my hand and...

"TADAAAAA! LOOK! I got a magical letter from SANTA yesterday - look! He has answered all of my questions! LOOK!"

Sarah Thomas snatched it hard from my hands and held it up high out of my reach.

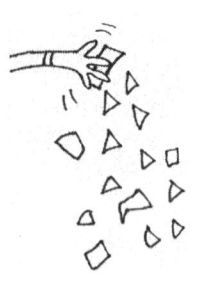

"From Santa? Really? Well if it's magical, then it'll magically go back to gather once I've done this then..."

She ripped it into tiny pieces, scattering it like wintery snow, blowing in the wind. The pieces blew all over the playground and settled onto the floor piece by piece, Sarah smirking the whole time.

I felt the fire rise up from my tummy, I tried to hold it in, but with sheer force it exploded out of me and somehow, I just felt myself lunging forward at her, pushing with all of my anger and she fell, with a look of horror on her face, right into the school pond.

 SPLASH!

The smell of the pond hit
me first, before any of the regret.

She howled, she cried, she coughed and spluttered and then Miss Jolly and the headteacher came storming our with a look of disbelief all over their faces!

"Eliza Greenwood - straight to my office! NOW YOUNG LADY!" he said

Miss Jolly escorted me there - she didn't say a word, just looked at me with a really disappointed look on her face.

Mum was called. Sarah's Parents were called.

I was in...

**So.
Much.
Trouble.**

I was told by Miss Jolly that I was lucky it was only detention for a week and lucky Sarah's parents were so forgiving and didn't want to take it further.

I had to apologise to Sarah who was soaked to the skin and stank of stale pond water.

Her smirk had long-gone, replaced with an angry, wet, face.
Sarah didn't even have to apologise for tearing up my letter! It didn't seem fair.

Nobody got to read the letter. There was no way of putting it all back together. Mum walked us home. Victor didn't dare look at me. He knows when to leave me alone.

Back at home, Mum made me a hot chocolate (her cure for everything) and we had one of her talks.

It involved her telling me all about how we need to look out for the people around us, how we need to

"Be kind to unkind people as there's often a reason for why they behave that way! Sometimes you don't know what other people are going through.

Choose kindness Eliza - always and don't retaliate if people push your buttons!

Your Dad was a gentle, kind, human and he would say the same to you, as I am now."

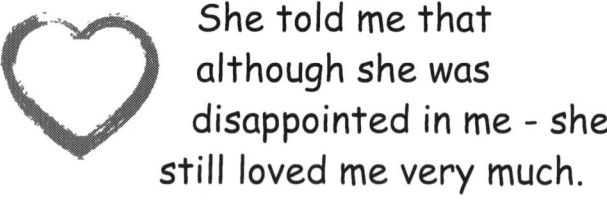

She told me that although she was disappointed in me - she still loved me very much.

It made me feel better, it also made me miss dad. I cried a bit more, then I did something I never thought I'd do. I decided to forgive Sarah.

☆ONE RUBBISH - THREE AWESOMES☆

One rubbish thing about today:

Everything

Three AWESOME things about today:

Even though it's been a bad day - there have been some awesomes.

1. Sarah fell into the pond (I know it's bad - but it was funny seeing her all soaked and smelling of pond water!)

2. Mum chats and cuddles with hot chocolate.

3. I got a unicorn badge in day 7 of my Biggle calendar today.

December 8th 2020

Today wasn't as bad as I thought it would be. I plucked up the courage to talk to Sarah and told her I was sorry (and I meant it,) for pushing her into the pond. She almost looked like she melted her icy-stare for a second, but it could've been a trick of the light.

Mr Marvin said he was very impressed with me for apologising again without being asked and that I showed *"responsibility and kindness"* and that he would tell the headteacher what I had done.

Detention actually wasn't all that bad! Not being forced out onto a freezing-cold playground to shiver for twenty

minutes, was actually quite nice!
I was warm in our classroom, it was peaceful and quiet and I was still allowed my snacks and told all this week, I had to read during my detention!

Reading is my favourite thing to do, so this detention business isn't that bad at all!
I am of course pretending it is awful though - otherwise I might be given another thing to do during detention instead!

Amalie missed me at playtime today and had to play with Clara and Jenny who she isn't super-keen on as they talk non-stop about make-up and phones. Yawn.

After school, mum made lasagne and although Victor moaned about it constantly, he actually ate every last bit and even had seconds!

At bedtime Mum sat on my bed and chatted to me about Sarah Thomas telling me *"Forgiveness is so much easier than hate - I'm so proud of you for forgiving Sarah! I know it's really hard to forgive - but choosing kindness is a really good thing to do!"*

The thing is - I am finding it really hard to mean it. Forgiveness is so hard! I'm using all the positive, happy-thoughts I can to keep smiling inside!

I'm so upset about the letter. I'm so upset nobody got a chance to read it and they think I just made the whole thing up. I'm super-cross that she told everyone that awful thing about Santa. I have this awful fire in my tummy and I try to blow it out, and I try to feel less cross - but I'm so upset about the whole thing - even though Santa **did** write to me, how can I prove he really did?

Maybe I should write another letter, or send him a Christmas card instead?

Are we allowed to write more than one letter? I guess I didn't send a wish-list the first time, just questions, and so maybe it doesn't actually count if it's a Christmas card?

I ask mum who tells me to sleep on it as *"things always feel so much better in the morning Eliza! Sometimes the biggest worries simply float away or shrink in the night!"*

☆ONE RUBBISH - THREE AWESOMES☆

One rubbish thing about today:

Everyone thinks my letter was made up.

Three AWESOME things about today:

1. Mr Marvin was pleased with me today and told the headteacher. (Detention still stands but that's OK as it's not that bad!)

2. Mum was proud of me

3. I got a squishy-bear pen in day 8 of my Biggle calendar today. I've wanted one of those for ages!

December 11th 2020

I've not written for a couple of days, as things have been pretty busy around here!

Mum has been working non-stop, so Nanna has been taking care of us mostly, even though Mum is worried about the whole Covid situation and us being at school, we could pass it to Nanna.

"Needs must" said Nanna.

I really love Nanna. She lets us have whatever we want for tea, doesn't push us to do our homework right away and lets us stay up late even on a school night.

We had a pretty big football match on Wednesday for **Galaxy girls.** I love playing for my hometown - it's so much fun and it's even better when we win! Dad loved taking me to football. Mum doesn't love it so much, but she comes to every game.

I got 'player of the match' for scoring a rather epic goal which took us into the lead 2 minutes from the end of the match. Our coach Tom, said he was really impressed!

I told Mr Marvin my trophy. Sarah said (in her usual whiny voice,) *"football is for boys - are you a boy Eliza?"* (everyone laughed!) Mr Marvin was really cross and told her that her attitude was very outdated and he would be speaking to her mum.

Jack Swan said he thought I was pretty good at football and invited me to play a match at playtime, which would have been totally brilliant if I didn't have detention all week.
In other news - everyone is excited about two things:

1. The school Christmas concert, which is online this year. This means I'll be less nervous as I won't be standing in front of hundreds of grown-ups, but mum says *"the magic isn't the same on a computer screen Eliza! I won't get to see yours and Victor's lovely faces clearly, or have the lovely PTA mulled wine!"* which made me giggle.

2. The school disco has been turned into an online disco! I am SO excited. We are all dressing up and will be on the online classrooms

video call, as a whole school together! There will be games and prizes too. Everyone is so excited as we thought there would be no Christmas party this year.

Mum said seeing as I always get a new outfit for all the usual Christmas parties, I could choose one online!

I have found a jumpsuit of dreams and although mum said *"That's more than a grown-up outfit costs! Blimey Eliza - I'll have to get more shifts in at work!"* she said I can still have it.

The biggest news I have, is that I've written Santa another letter and I'm hoping he replies again.

If he does - I am keeping it in my pocket and inviting only those I trust (not Sarah Thomas,) to look at it a playtime.

I have put it by the fireplace tonight before bed and am hoping it gets sucked up the chimney like the others.

Mum says it might not, because you only really get a one-letter-chance each year, because Santa has an awful lot of letters to get through.

Dear Santa and Duke

Thank you for writing back to me. I know you are very busy and I didn't want to bother you again - but a girl at school tore up your letter and nobody believes I even had a reply from you.

Santa - I truly still believe in you, but so many of my friends don't and it's making me feel so cross and sad. What can I do to help them believe?

It also makes me sad that not everyone can have the same at Christmas and some have very little at all. What can be done about that? The shops are emptying with what my mum says is 'panic buying' which seems very silly and selfish to me Santa. What can be done?

Love,

Eliza Greenwood.

While I really do understand Santa is a busy man - I think he really needs to help me with my worries about other kids not having enough.

This Covid Christmas Crisis is serious! So many shops have sold out of basic things and mum says it's because,

"people get scared and silly Eliza! I don't think people are inherently selfish and bad - they just worry, so they panic and buy more than they actually need.

In turn - others copy and before you know it there isn't enough for everyone!"

It's making me worry like it did last time. I wish Covid would go away.

I hope Santa replies to my letter.

☆ONE RUBBISH - THREE AWESOMES☆

One rubbish thing about ~~today~~ **the last few days:**

The panic buying is really worrying me.

Three AWESOME things about ~~today~~ **the last few days:**

1. We won our footy match and I was 'player of the match' and can keep the trophy now until after Christmas as there's no more games until January.

2. Mum has ordered the 'jumpsuit of dreams!'

3. The Biggle calendar has had some epic offerings over the last few days, including - a glitter keyring!

December 12th 2020

The letter has gone! **OMG!** This means he has accepted it! (Or one of our dogs ate it?)

Today, after our bore-chores, Mum surprised us with a 'drive in' Christmas movie! In America they do this all the time, but here in the UK we don't usually have outdoor cinemas!

We took our lovely old camper-van and mum made us hot chocolate at the little table. She put the fan-heater on so we didn't freeze!

It was one of our family all-time-favourite Christmas movies that Dad absolutely loved. **'Miracle on 34th street!'**

Dad used to joke that our Grandad was the actor who played Santa in the movie and we believed him, that was until I read about the actor, in one of Victor's 'know everything' encyclopaedias he got for Christmas one year.

The actor was actually the brother of a famous TV wildlife expert and not our grandad at all. Silly old Dad!

Dad always joked about stuff like that. Mum used to roll her eyes but we thought he was super-funny. I miss his silly jokes.

The movie was as brilliant as always (if you've never seen it you really should!)

 The little girl was a bit like me - she believed in Santa but her mummy didn't (she didn't sound like a very nice mummy to me!)

Anyway, in the end - well, I won't spoil it because mum says it's mean to spoil the endings of movies for people who haven't watch them. (Spoiler alert! It's mushy and lovely and happy and made mum cry... AGAIN!)

At the movies, because of Covid, we weren't allowed out of the van - which was O.K because we have our own loo! Lucky, because Victor always needs to go twenty-million times at the movies, and it is SO annoying, as I usually have to take him!

☆ONE RUBBISH - THREE AWESOMES☆

One rubbish thing about today:

Nothing! Even the bore-chores weren't that bad!

Three AWESOME things about today:

1. The letter has gone!

2. We went to the drive-in movies

3. Victor video-called Arthur for a virtual play-date from late afternoon until bedtime so I got to watch whatever I wanted to on TV in peace! YAY!

December 13th 2020

ELEVEN sleeps until Christmas eve. Come on Santa you are cutting this fine! No reply yet. Please reply.

Mum said we could have a PJ day today as she was so tired. She's been working really hard lately and Nanna has been around a lot.

Nanna says Mum *"needs to be home more and at work less - otherwise she will burn out!*

Mum says if she doesn't work, *"who will pay the bills? The money fairies?"*

I don't like the idea of mum 'burning out' all and think I need to talk to her. I'm wondering if 'money fairies' are real - this could be the solution to the Covid Christmas Crisis.

 Amalie video called me today to show me she had lost the last of her front teeth today. She is the last in our year to loose them and once, at school, Sarah Thomas said it's because Amalie is *"A great big baby with baby teeth"* This made Amalie cry and made me get that fire in my tummy again.

Before I could say anything, Mr Marvin said that Sarah must apologise and that actually, *"Amalie is lucky because the later they fall out, the better for her big teeth! It has nothing at all to do with being a baby."*

I really don't like it when Amalie, or anybody I care about cry. It makes me feel like crying too.

Mum says
 *"that's a good thing called 'empathy' Eliza -it means you understand and

share the feelings of others, it means you are a really nice little human my lovely Eliza!"

I really like it when mum says stuff like that. It makes me feel warm and happy.

It makes me feel like I'm really good!

I like feeling that way.

It makes me want to do more things that make me feel good. It gives me a really big brain wave and light-bulb moment!

I might need a bit (actually - a lot,) of help to pull my idea off though.

I'm going to talk to mum about it in the morning.

☆ONE RUBBISH - THREE AWESOMES☆

One rubbish thing about today:

Still no reply from the man in red.

Three AWESOME things about today:

1. Amalie's tooth finally fell out.

2. Mum said I was a really nice person, because I care about others when they are sad.

3. I've had an idea how to make Christmas better for everyone!

December 14th 2020

Last night after mum said the nice things...

I had 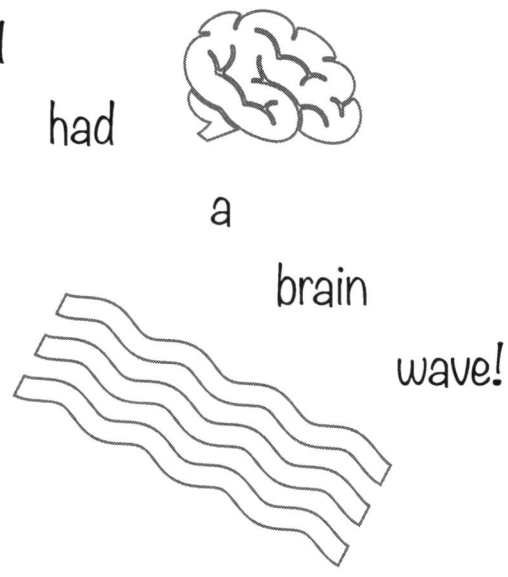 a brain wave!

If Santa is super-busy (which I know he is) with all the kids gifts and orders from parents and deliveries and managing elves and well, all the Christmassy Santa things, then maybe I could help him?

One of the things I worry about most, is the kids who don't have as much as everyone else.

The kids who don't actually have anything at all, not even meals, especially now since the pandemic.

How will they even have Christmas dinner?

Mum says some parents lost their jobs, some couldn't work because there was no school and had to look after their children instead so don't have as much money now.

Mum said some parents got really sick and still can't work like Miss Jolly's boyfriend. This makes me so sad. I didn't even know her boyfriend had been so poorly. Poor Miss Jolly - she isn't grumpy, she's just really sad and worried..

I'm going to do something to make things just that little bit better for those in need. I'm going to need lots of help from Mum, Victor and the school, but I really think we could sort out this Covid Christmas Crisis - even just a little bit, so tonight, before bed, with Mum's help, I emailed Mr Marvin...

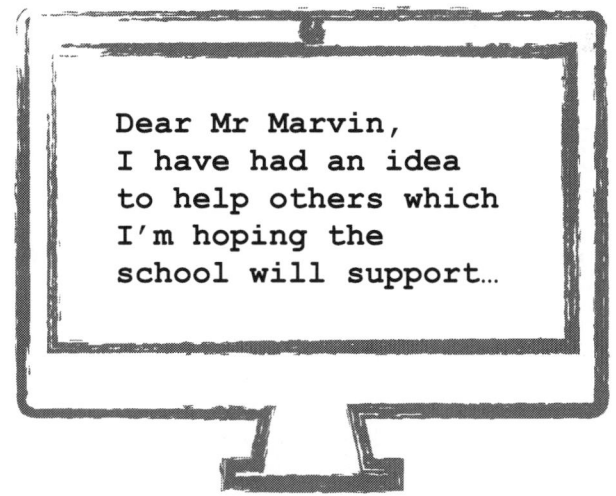

Dear Mr Marvin,
I have had an idea
to help others which
I'm hoping the
school will support...

I was really nervous and worried what to say, but mum helped me put it all nicely, and spell-check on mum's fancy computer, meant none of my spelling was wrong! Yay!

> If we all brought a festive box or basket into school, filled with either Christmas food or suitable gifts for different aged children - we could then donate them to those less fortunate than ourselves.

I was so worried that Mr Marvin and the headteacher would think it a silly idea and would say no, and I almost didn't send it until mum said,

"Eliza Greenwood - you have a heart

of gold and a brain full of wonderful ideas. If anyone says no to your ideas, it doesn't mean those ideas are silly or not good enough! There are many reasons people say no to children and grow-ups too! If you don't at least try - how will you ever know?"

Mum always knows just what to say.

I finished up my email and pressed SEND...

```
I can't really do this on my
own and need a bit of help. I
hope you will say yes to my
idea because time is running
out - it'll soon be Christmas
and so many will be without -
this really is a Covid
Christmas Crisis Mr Marvin.

Best wishes, Eliza
```

☆ONE RUBBISH - THREE AWESOMES☆

One rubbish thing about today:

Year 4 are out of isolation. I feel really sad about Miss Jolly.

Three AWESOME things about today:

1. I've had the most brilliant idea!

2. I bought Mum, Nanna and Victor's presents today, online, with Mum's help. (She's been giving us 'virtual pocket money since lockdown in March. We write down in the diary how much we have used and we can spend it online!)

3. My jumpsuit of dreams arrived and it is AMAZING! I love it!

December 15th 2020

Got to school late again (Mum's phone ran out of batteries which we all rely on as an alarm!)

Miss Jolly - again was VERY UN-JOLLY and embarrassed me in front of the whole class saying that if I like to be late - I won't mind being late to lunch today while I help her sort the MESSIEST CLOAKROOM EVER!

I understand how when you are upset it can make you a bit snappy, so I don't bite back, and instead I apologise, then at lunchtime, I make the cloakroom the tidiest it's ever been. I also draw her a lovely picture and leave it on her desk.

After lunchtime she sees it and she ACTUALLY SMILES!

Today in assembly, Mr Marvin and the headteacher, asked me to stand up in front of everyone.

MY HEART WAS BEATING

OUT

OF

MY

CHEST...

My mouth went so dry.

Mr Marvin said,

"Last night I received an email from Eliza Greenwood and her mother. Eliza has had the kindest, most wonderful idea, and as a school we would like you to all support this wonderful idea!"

I feel a flush of red move up my cheeks and tingle the back of my neck.

My heart flutters and goosebumps prickled my arms. I feel an enormous sense of happiness all around me, like being hugged by stars and hearts!

I feel amazing. I also feel like I'll puke at any minute with nerves, as

ALL eyes are on ME!

Mr Marvin told them all about my festive basket and box ideas.

A hum of excitement went around the room and ended only when Mrs Marston played the introduction to Jingle bells on the piano, indicating it was time to stop talking and start singing!

Even Miss Jolly was smiling again and gave me a wink! Magic was in the air!

☆ONE RUBBISH - THREE AWESOMES☆

One rubbish thing about today:

NOTHING!

Three AWESOME things about today:

1. EVERYTHING!

2. EVERYTHING!

3. EVERYTHING!

December 16th 2020

Santa comes in 8 sleeps time. I have a lot of work to do to help him. Still no reply by the way, but weirdly - it's not upsetting me as I am **SO VERY BUSY** with all the organisation of my festive baskets and boxes.

Mrs Jones' parents own a green-grocers and have kindly donated 45 wooden crates for us to use! Mum has painted little festive things on them, like Robins and holly and they look AMAZING!

Nanna said Mum is *"burning the candle at both ends and will burn out soon if she's not careful!"*

I do worry about all this burning Nanna mentions. Mum said it's an *"old people worry Eliza, I am fine and won't really burn out! It's just a funny phrase meaning, if you do too much you'll be very tired indeed!"*

That makes me feel a lot better that she's not going to burn anytime soon and I start making signs for the school gates for people to drop their donations off.

Mr Marvin says the bike shed is a good place to put them incase it rains (or snows! I really hope it snows this Christmas because it is one of my most favourite things!)

Tomorrow is the first day of box and basket drop-offs. We are doing it over 3 days so it gives us time to get them delivered to those in need. I'm so nervous - what if nobody joins in? What if we don't have enough?
"Oh but what if it goes crazy and you get so, so many Eliza!" says mum. And I truly hope she is right.

☆ONE RUBBISH - THREE AWESOMES☆

One rubbish thing about today:

NOTHING!

Three AWESOME things about today:

1. Mum let me stay up late decorating boxes with her while 'Elf' the movie was on in the background. Even on a school night!

2. Victor cleaned his room and found my old glitter pen that I thought was lost forever.

3. In my Biggle calendar today I got a Santa keyring. I think this is a sign!

December 17th 2020

Today was THE best day

EVER!

I am so happy! Not only did everyone in the entire school bring a wrapped gift box full of loveliness or a basket of festive food - some brought in **two or three!!!**

This means we now have over 500 baskets and boxes for families in need this Christmas.

Take that Covid! You can't stop the spirit of Christmas!

Mr Marvin was so pleased but also totally shocked and a little worried how we were going to deliver all of the boxes to families in need.

Luckily, Amalie's dad has a big van and offered to help us get them all to the local charities that help families.

Mr Marvin said I could choose **three** special helpers to come with us on the school bus, which we also filled with the baskets and boxes. It meant we got the whole afternoon off school, so you can imagine how many kids put their hands up in the air, desperate for me to pick them! Sarah Thomas included.

I chose Amalie (of course!) Then I chose Victor and his friend Arthur from the year below us, because Victor was looking at me with his big blue eyes all shiny and cute. Now I know why he gets away with so much with mum!

It took FOREVER to load up the van and school mini-bus, even with a human chain made up of all of year 6! It was so much fun, but very hard work.

The headteacher said we'd all get extra break tomorrow for our efforts! How cool is that?!

Amalie's dad drove the van with Amalie in the front. Mum, me, Victor and Arthur went with Mr Marvin on the school bus. His driving was worse than Dad's used to be and made me feel a bit squiffy.

We stopped off at 4 local charities and each one was more thankful than the last. They count believe how much stuff we'd managed to collect.

On the very last drop, the lady at the charity 'helpful families' told us our donations were,

 "Just in time! We've hundreds families really struggling at the moment who have nothing for their children for Christmas and nothing special to eat on Christmas day! You are a real angel young   lady!"

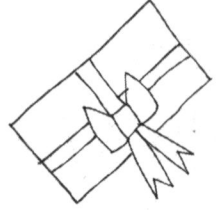

This made mum cry, and Mr Marvin wasn't sure what to do. It was a bit embarrassing!

The lady told us the boxes all had to be in quarantine for 72 hours to be safe from spreading coronavirus (Mum told me quarantine means 'keeping something in once place and not being touched by others to prevent the spread of disease!')

A man from the local paper took our photo and told us it would be Friday's FRONT PAGE news! Wow! I can just picture Sarah Thomas' face when she sees my face on the front page of the

Star News!

Today doesn't feel real - it feels like a lovely dream. I just wish Dad was here to see it all.

Friday 18th December

Not only was it fish and chip Friday today, after school it was

THE EPIC SCHOOL ONLINE DISCO!

I ran home from school as fast as my legs would take me. I ran into the house, up the stairs (shouting a quick hello to mum, as I passed her on the stairs) and got into my 'jumpsuit of dreams' in 10 seconds flat.

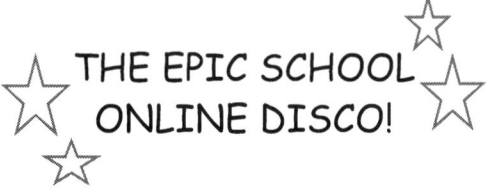

I brushed my hair and my teeth and called mum to do my hair. She used her hair straighteners to make my hair long and straight. (I'm not being a show-off or anything - but I think I looked pretty good!)

Mum cried, again. She said *"Oh Eliza you are growing up so fast! You look so beautiful - I do wish your dad was here to see you now!"*

Victor opted for his best jeans and a Christmas shirt that had Christmas puddings printed all over. He spiked his hair up and put one of dad's old bow ties on. Mum cried again.

Why do grow-ups get SO emotional about us growing up? Of course we grow up - that's what we are supposed to do!

The online disco started at 6pm and was full of our favourite Christmas songs. The last song 'Last Christmas' - everyone waved their glow sticks to in the dark. Then, at precisely 745.pm, just before the disco was about to end, something incredible happened, but I'm saving that for tomorrow's diary entry. It's too much for one day.

☆ONE RUBBISH - THREE AWESOMES☆

One rubbish thing about today:

NOTHING!

Three AWESOME things about today:

1. I don't know where to begin!

2. Absolutely everything

3. Just everything!

Friday 19th December.

I can't even begin. I don't know where to start.

Last night feels like a crazy dream.

It all started with the school Christmas online disco. The games were so much fun, there were our favourite chart tracks and Christmas songs to dance to. Even mum did her 90's rave moves and we weren't even that embarrassed! That's how much fun we were having!

Then...

At 7.45pm, just as the D.J was winding down the party for the 8pm finish, something incredible happened.

Everyone stopped dancing. One by one they were pointing at our screen...

Pointing at us! They were staring in amazement, coming closer to their screens to try and get a better look at whatever it was they were pointing at.

I started to blush - my cheeks bright red and my heart beating fast...

Had my jumpsuit come undone? Did I have party food on my face? Had my hair gone sweaty with all the dancing? Were mum's dance moves really **that** awful?

They were pointing and shouting....

"LOOK! Eliza Look!"

Slowly, mum, Victor and I turned around...

There was **nothing** there!

By now everyone was hysterical - jumping around, some had turned their mics on and were screaming with delight...

WHAT ON EARTH HAD THEY SEEN?

Mum started to get a bit panicked - was there someone in the house? She told us to wait in the front room while she checked the entire house.

Nothing.

Everyone was shouting - now they ALL had their mics on and the sound was so loud we couldn't make out what they were saying!

Then mum's phone rang and she just went quiet.

"It's Amalie's mum" Mum said, a bewildered expression across her face,

"she's saying that everyone saw Santa behind us. Just for a brief moment. He was right there, surrounded by... What did you say? Hold on I can't hear you... Eliza turn the sound down on the computer..."

I turned off the sound and turned back to mum eager to hear more. By now Arthur was running around the house shouting *"Santa! Santa! Santa!"*

Mum looked at me, shocked and silent..

"She says he appeared behind us - he waved, he was surrounded by sparkly-gold starlight. He kept waving and smiling and then he was gone!"

It took so long for everyone to calm down. Mr Marvin told everyone to calm down and log out from their computers. Mum poured herself a glass of wine and made us hot chocolate and we sat chatting about what had happened!

Some in my class started saying it was a trick, on the class chat group.

That somehow we had projected an image behind us, but anyone who knows my mum knows she is the least tech-wiz person on the planet! How would we even do that?

When we woke up this morning, mum let us skip our usual Saturday chores in favour of Christmas movies and leftover party food.

We couldn't focus on the movie. Mum's phone was ringing all day with the newspapers and TV stations wanting to talk to us!

Someone had taken a screenshot of the online disco and shared it on social media.

The school had sent an email of apology, because people are not allowed to share photos of kids online without parental permission, and yet our faces with Santa behind us was now trending all over the world, and all over the front page of the tabloids!

with all the attention of Santa's appearance, also came the story of the festive boxes and baskets.

The lady from 'Helpful Families' was on the lunchtime news saying what an angel I was and that,

"All the gifts mean lots of children will be incredibly happy this year! She really is a Christmas dream come true!"

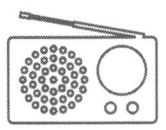

On all the radio stations, instead of the usual doomy-gloomy Covid reports, it was all about Santa and the magic of Christmas! People were sharing their own stories of how they had seen Santa over the years. From a sighting in Surfers Paradise on the Gold Coast, to a sighting in Kwethluk, Alaska, people were sharing their own sightings and magical stories of Father Christmas!

Social media was flooded with pictures and photos and stories using a hashtag #IBelieveInSanta

And it just felt like all of the awful sadness and stress of this really tricky year, slipped away for a while.

Then something really, TRULY wonderful happened...

People from all over the world, started making their **own** baskets of Christmas food and boxes of gifts for children and taking them to their local charities and shelters in need.

Mum couldn't stop crying (again!)

"Do you see what you have done Eliza my little darling girl? You have given hope to so many.

You have made others think like you do! I am SO proud of you!"

The last 24 hours have been crazy!

☆ONE RUBBISH - THREE AWESOMES☆

One rubbish thing about today:

NOTHING!

Three AWESOME things about today:

1. Mum is proud of me

2. Everyone around the world is giving gifts and food to those in need.

3. Covid Christmas Crisis = SORTED!

December 24th 2020

It's been a really, crazy, busy few days talking to radio stations and doing the awesome online school concert, (yes - mum cried again!) And then the school Christmas holidays began!

Yesterday it started snowing and Victor and I got to go sledging with Amalie and Arthur! It was EPIC! Dad would have loved it so much!

We built a snowman too, then had hot chocolate from a flask that Amalie's mum had brought with her.

It's now Christmas eve and everything has been truly magical this last few days. It still feels like a dream, a really fabulous, happy dream.

I wish dad was here. It's really hard without him - especially at Christmas and it really hurts.

Mum says it's O.K to feel sad - even in really happy times, and to keep writing all of my feelings down in my **'thinky-thoughts'** journal, as it really helps to get those feelings out and onto paper.

I do find writing helps me feel better, and I know when one day, maybe when I'm all grown-up, I won't look back on this Covid year as **ALL BAD**, but see the good things that happened too.

Mum said *"Eliza, when bad things happen, it is easy to feel bad all the time, to see all the sadness in the world and feel dark inside - but you have to keep looking for the light and the happy, and the love, and all the good that people do."*

Mum always knows just what to say.

Tonight, before heading up to bed, we left carrots for the reindeer.

We also left dad's old whiskey in a glass for Santa (although mum is very concerned about Santa drinking and driving - dad always insisted Santa liked whiskey way more than milk!)

Our stockings are hung by the fireplace and I'm writing this as usual, all tucked up in bed.

Victor is already asleep and I can hear the chattering from the TV downstairs and I feel safe and cosy.

I can't believe tomorrow is Christmas day! I am SO excited! I love Christmas day so much - not just the presents, but all of it. The movies on TV, the sweets, the Christmas dinner and Christmas pudding (I LOVE Christmas pudding) and the late night we are allowed because it's Christmas.

Tonight I am going to try and stay awake as long as possible to see Santa. I try every year but fail miserably. Mum says I have Dad's ability for always falling asleep quickly.

☆ONE RUBBISH - THREE AWESOMES☆

One rubbish thing about today:

NOTHING!

Three AWESOME things about today:

1. Mum let us stay up a little later to make cookies for Santa

2. I'm so excited that it's Christmas Eve!

3. Santa is coming tonight!

December 25th 2020

I am trying to write this without shaking! Today just topped ~~the whole of December.~~ Actually scrap that...

Today just topped the whole **YEAR!** (Take that COVID you slime-ball of nasty!)

After waking up and running in to wake mum (super-early of course!) We all went downstairs. Victor actually ran down and mum shouted that we didn't want to end up in A&E on Christmas day and to please slow down!

Under the tree were a few presents wrapped beautifully.

Our stockings were full of amazing things like crayons and books and juggling balls and felt-tip pens and at the bottom of mine, was a rolled up note, wrapped with bright red ribbon...

Dear Eliza,

Sometimes it can take something really bad to happen, to see the good in the world.

It has been a really hard year for so many families Eliza, including your own, and yet you have shown such resilience and kindness, and for that you should be so proud of yourself. I know your dad would be very proud of you.

In answer to your question about getting people to believe in me, I'm afraid that is something that each and every person has to do for themselves. It takes a lot of faith to believe in something you can't see - and sometimes, even when people do see things they struggle to believe.
You have to not worry about what others believe or think and focus on your own dreams and beliefs. To believe in yourself and what you can achieve is the real magic Eliza - and look at what that belief in yourself did this Christmas! You made the world come together and help those in need and that is the true spirit of Christmas. Real magic Eliza!

Merry Christmas my little helper!

                Love Santa xx

For the first time, in a very long time, I cried happy-for-what-I-have-tears.

I know that sounds super-mushy, but I really am happy for what I have, because although I miss my dad so very much, I am lucky to have a brilliant mum and brother (yes - I even love YOU Victor if you are reading this!)

Like Santa said in his very first letter to me 'he still lives on in me always. Every time I think of a happy memory - he is right there in my heart and with me always.'

I've decided that I'm not going to just do this special thing as a one-off. I'm actually going to do it every year and although it might not be as magical year after year, and maybe not as many will join in and help me, I'll keep on going and keep helping others because like Santa says - that is the true spirit of Christmas.

It's not about the gifts under the tree or sweets and treats (although those are REALLY nice And yes - I did get the style doll and she has pink hair and a little denim outfit and is the most wonderful doll you ever did see.)

Christmas is about spending time with those you love and remembering hose who aren't with you anymore, and, if you can, helping those less fortunate than yourself.

I'm going to end this journal here now - even though there's a few days left until the end of the year.

Maybe someone else would like to fill it with their own Christmas Thinky-

Thoughts if they find it one day, (and that includes you Victor - maybe you'd like to write your feelings down, because I never really stopped to think how much you must miss dad too.)

I'll start my new journal on January 1st, 2021 with a great big positive smile, using my BRAND NEW Unicorn pen that Victor bought me for Christmas with his pocket money.

2021 might be brilliant, or it might be tricky again.

Whatever happens, I know as long as I have my family and friends, as long as I write down my feelings and keep chatting with mum - I'll find the positives and know that even when things get tough - there is still so much to be thankful for.

Eliza xx

☆ONE RUBBISH - THREE AWESOMES☆

One rubbish thing about today:

NOTHING!

Three AWESOME things about today:

1. I feel so lucky to have my lovely family.

2. I got the pink style doll and she is wonderful.

3. I feel really, truly, happy. Merry Christmas!

My Thinky-Thoughts

☆ONE RUBBISH - THREE AWESOMES☆

One rubbish thing about today:

Three AWESOME things about today:

1.

2.

3.

My Thinky-Thoughts

☆ONE RUBBISH - THREE AWESOMES☆

One rubbish thing about today:

Three AWESOME things about today:

1.

2.

3.

My Thinky-Thoughts

☆ONE RUBBISH - THREE AWESOMES☆

One rubbish thing about today:

Three AWESOME things about today:

1.

2.

3.

My Thinky-Thoughts

☆ONE RUBBISH - THREE AWESOMES☆

One rubbish thing about today:

Three AWESOME things about today:

1.

2.

3.

My Thinky-Thoughts

☆ONE RUBBISH - THREE AWESOMES☆

One rubbish thing about today:

Three AWESOME things about today:

1.

2.

3.

My Thinky-Thoughts

☆ONE RUBBISH - THREE AWESOMES☆

One rubbish thing about today:

Three AWESOME things about today:

1.

2.

3.

 # Always choose kindness...

The characters in this book are fictional, but are based on three wonderful little humans that live in a leafy little town in the Midlands, UK.

Very special kids with hearts of gold. One called Evie, who a couple of years ago, while still at primary school, set up #ShoeboxesForRefugees to help local refugees have a little something special for Christmas.

Another special little girl called Amalie, during lockdown 2020, used her mum's sewing machine to make over 100 face masks to sell locally and spent most of the profits to buy donations for food banks, to help families in need during lockdown.

finally, a little girl called Betsy, who on hearing school meals would be cancelled during school holidays, asked her headteacher if they could have an 'own clothes day at school' and in exhale everybody brings in a tin of food which was then donated to the local food bank.

I hope this book inspires other little humans to do good in the world. Even the smallest thing can make a big difference.

About the Author

Fi Star-Stone is a parenting advisor and author who lives in the Midlands with her two children, husband, two dogs and two cats.

Likes: Moomins, Cake, Movies, Dog walks and kitchen dancing.

Dislikes: Very early mornings and unkind people.

Favourite Music: The Killers, Pink, and David Bowie.

The boring bit you have to put on books...

Copyright © 2020 Fi Star-Stone

All rights reserved. No part of this publication, including the illustrations may be reproduced, distributed, or transmitted in any form or by any means, including photocopying, recording, or other electronic or mechanical methods, without the prior written permission of the publisher and author except in the case of brief quotations embodied in reviews and certain other noncommercial uses permitted by copyright law. For permission requests, write to the author Fi Star-Stone at fistarstone@gmail.com

Any spelling or grammatical errors in this book are entirely intentional as they are written in character as 10 year old Eliza Greenwood ;-)

Printed in Great Britain
by Amazon